Moonbeam

by Sharma Krauskopf

illustrated by Naomi Howland

 Richard C. Owen Publishers, Inc.
Katonah, New York

One summer night long ago
in the Highlands of Scotland,
the Moon Princess got lost.

She could not find her
way back to her castle
in the Glen of Light.

The Moon Princess wandered around
for hours and hours.
Her soft shoes became wet and worn.
Her fine clothes snagged and tore on thistles
and thorns.

5

The Moon Princess grew tired and weary.
Just when she felt that she could go no farther,
she saw a large, dark shape in the fog.

6

The shape came closer and closer,
and out of the fog stepped a big, black cow.

The great beast stopped before the Moon Princess.
"I am lost," sobbed the Moon Princess.
"Please help me find my way home."

The gentle beast sank to its knees
so the Moon Princess could climb up
on its back.

The great black cow carried the princess
across the land to the steps of her castle
in the Glen of Light.

The Moon Queen was overjoyed
to see her daughter.
She was most grateful for her return.

The Moon Queen took a softly glowing moonbeam
and fastened it around the great, black cow's middle.
"Your family will be forever honored by this belt,"
she told the cow.

13

And so today in fields and meadows,
you may see black Beltie cows
with the soft, white color of glowing moonbeams
around their middles.

photo of Misty Isle courtesy of Sharma Krauskopf

Nonfiction Note

The Belted Galloway is an ancient breed of cattle from the stony hills, heathery mountains, and fertile glens of the cold, damp, windy coastal district of Scotland. Though rare, there are about 8,000 Belties in the United States. Belties have thick coats of hair, fuzzy ears, and shaggy bangs. They are long lived, docile, and courageous. Belties are beef cows and are not raised for their milk. They are often called *Oreo Cookie cows* because of their unique black and white color combination.